This Book Belongs To

_____

The Wind in the Willows

HOME SWEET HOME

Based on the original story by Kenneth Grahame

Retold by Andrea Stacy Leach
Illustrated by Holly Hannon

McClanahan Book Company, Inc.
New York

Rat and Mole were returning home after a day's outing. They were walking along a familiar path. It was mid-December and night was falling fast. A bit of powdery snow lay on the ground.

"It looks as if we are coming to a village," said the Mole with some uncertainty.

"Oh, never mind!" said the Water Rat. "At this season of the year they're all safe indoors, sitting around the fire. Men, women, and children, dogs and cats and all. We shall slip through all right without any bother."

"And we can have a look at them through their windows if you like, and see what they are doing."

The two spectators felt homesick as they watched through the windows. They saw a cat being stroked, a sleepy child carried to bed, and a tired old man stretch and light his pipe.

Once beyond the windows of the village, they plodded along silently on the last stretch home. Rat was walking a little ahead, and did not notice that the Mole had stopped suddenly.

"Please stop, Ratty!" pleaded the Mole. "I've just come across the smell of my old home and I must go to it. Please come back!"

The rat was too far ahead to hear what the

Mole was saying. Rat called back that they must not stop yet.

The Mole felt a big sob gathering low inside him. With an effort, he caught up with Rat who began chattering cheerfully about making supper and a roaring fire when they got back.

The Mole sat sadly on a tree stump, unable to hold back his tears anymore. Rat was astonished and dismayed. He patted Mole gently on the shoulder. "What is it, old friend? Whatever can be the matter?"

Mole could hardly speak. "I know it's a— shabby, dingy little place—not like your cozy quarters—but it was my own little house, and I was fond of it—and I went away and forgot all about it. Then I smelled it and I called, but you wouldn't listen."

Rat waited until Mole stopped crying. "We're going to find that home of yours, old friend. Cheer up, take my arm, and soon we'll be back there again."

They walked in silence for a little while. Then Mole stood rigid a moment, his uplifted nose quivering faintly. He nosed his way over a field, open and bare in the faint starlight.

Suddenly, without giving any warning, the

Mole dived. The Rat promptly followed Mole down through the dark tunnel to which his nose had led him.

It seemed a long time to Rat before the passage ended, and he could stand erect and shake himself. The Mole struck a match. Directly facing them was his little front door with "Mole End" painted over the doorbell at the side.

The Mole hurried Rat through the door, lit a lamp in the hall, and took one glance around his old home.

He saw the dust lying thick on everything. He saw the cheerless, deserted look of the long-neglected house and its worn, shabby contents—and collapsed on a hall chair, his nose in his paws.

"Oh Ratty!" he cried dismally, "Why ever did I do it? Why did I bring you to this cold little place on a night like this? You might have been at River Bank by this time, toasting your toes before a blazing fire, with all your own nice things around you!"

The Rat paid no attention. He was running
here and there opening doors, inspecting rooms
and cupboards, and lighting lamps and candles.

"Old friend, what a splendid house this is!" Rat called out cheerily. "So compact, everything here and in its place. The first thing we want is a good fire."

Encouraged by Rat, the Mole roused himself and dusted and polished with energy. The Rat ran to and fro with armfuls of wood and soon had a cheerful fire going.

But soon Mole felt depressed again. "Rat," he moaned, "how about your supper, you poor, hungry animal? I've nothing to give you—not even a crumb!"

"Get moving," said Rat. "Come with me and look."

They found a tin of sardines, a box of cookies, and a German sausage wrapped in silver paper.

"There's a banquet for you," said Rat as he set the table. Then he headed for the cellar and reappeared with a bottle of soda in each paw and another under each arm.

They had just gone to work with the
sardine-opener when sounds were heard
outside—sounds like the scuffling of small feet
in gravel and a confused murmur of tiny voices.

"I think it must be the field mice," said the
Mole. "They go around singing carols at this
time of year. They come to Mole End last of all.
I used to give them hot drinks and supper too."

"That sounds wonderful, Mole. Let's have a

look at them!" cried the Rat, jumping up and running to the door.

It was a pretty sight. Outside the door, lit by the rays of a lantern, stood eight or ten little field mice.

As the door opened, one of the older ones that carried the lantern was just saying, "Now then, one, two, three!" Immediately their shrill voices rose in the air, singing an old-time carol.

"Very well sung, boys!" cried the Rat when the voices ceased. "And now come in and warm yourselves by the fire, and have something hot!"

"Yes, come along," cried the Mole eagerly. "This is just like old times...just a minute—oh, Ratty! We've nothing to give them!"

"You leave that to me," said the Rat.

"Are there any stores open at this hour of the night?" Rat asked the field mouse who sat in front of the dimly lit lantern.

"Certainly, sir," replied the field mouse. Rat handed him some coins and a large basket, and the field mouse hurried to the store.

When he returned, he emptied his purchases onto the table, and in a very few minutes supper was ready.

As they sat down to supper, Mole saw his friends' faces brighten and beam. What a happy homecoming it had turned out to be, after all.

When the door closed on the last of the field mice, Mole and Rat pulled up their chairs to the fire and discussed the events of the day.

"Mole, I'm ready to drop," Rat said. "I'll take this bunk. What a jolly place this is!"

Mole agreed. He did not want to abandon his new life, but it was good to think he had this to come back to, this place which was all his own.